Dog's
ABC

Text and illustrations copyright © 2000 by Tucker Slingsby Ltd

All rights reserved.

Devised and produced by Tucker Slingsby Ltd

Berkeley House, London

CIP Data is available.

Published in the United States 2002 by Dutton Children's Books,
a division of Penguin Putnam Books for Young Readers
345 Hudson Street, New York, New York 10014
www.penguinputnam.com

Typography by Jason Henry

Printed in Mexico.

First American Edition
2 4 6 8 10 9 7 5 3 1
ISBN 0-525-46837-4

Dutton Children's Books · New York

Dog's ABC

A Silly Story About the Alphabet

by Emma Dodd

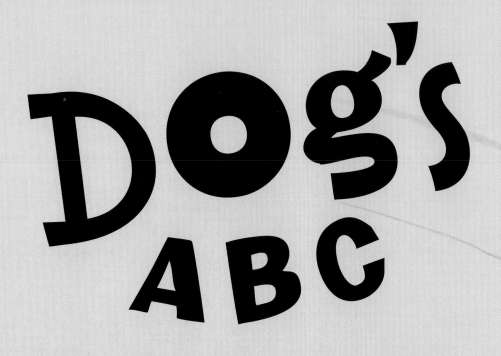

Aa APPLE

Dog loves adventure, but he doesn't always know where to find it.

Bonk!

An apple falls on his head. Dog barks, and a bird flies out of the apple tree.

Bb BIRD

A cat runs after the bird.
That gives Dog an idea.

Cc CAT

He plays chase, too.

Woof! barks Dog.

He chases the cat away.

Dd DOG

The bird flies back to her nest and sits on her eggs. That was a good adventure, thinks Dog.

Now it is time for a nap. Just then, a frog croaks loudly. **Ribbit!**

Ee EGGS

Ff FROG

Dog chases the frog over
the gate...

Gg GATE

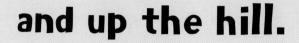

and up the hill.

Whew!

**Now Dog is very hot
and tired.**

Hh HILL

He stops to rest.

Buzz!

An insect lands
on his nose and
stings him.

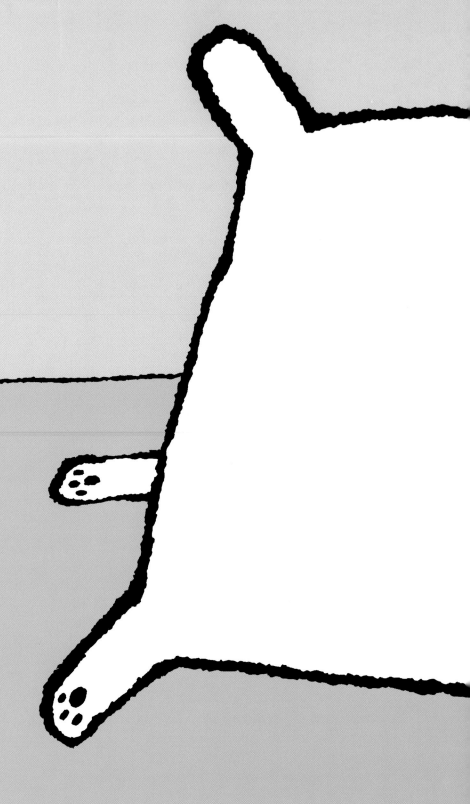

 **Ii** INSECT

Ouch!

It makes Dog jump.

Jj JUMP

Dog's nose hurts.
Only one thing
will make him
feel better....

Kk KITCHEN

Dog runs into the kitchen as fast as his little legs can carry him.

Dog gobbles his meal.

Mm MEAL

His nose still hurts. Dog looks for some cold water. He tries to put his nose in the fishbowl, but his nose is too big.

The two orange fish in the bowl blow bubbles at Dog.

Nn NOSE

Dog goes back outside.
He dips his nose in the pond.

Ahhhh...

much better.

Pp POND

Enough adventure, thinks Dog.
He curls up to nap. But the ducks are
too noisy.

Qq QUACK

Dog is too tired to chase them.
And then it begins to rain.

Rr RAIN

The sky is dark.

Achoo!

Dog sneezes and shakes the water out of his coat.

Ss SKY

He stands under a tree, but he still gets wet.

Tt TREE

Dog sees an umbrella
coming toward him.

Uu UMBRELLA

Under the umbrella
is his friend Vicky.

"Time to go home,"
she says.

Vv VICKY

Dog dashes into the house,
dripping water on the rug.
He is extremely tired.

Ww WATER

Xx E<u>X</u>TREMELY

He gives a great big yawn.

Hurray!

It is time for a nap!

Yy YAWN

Dog thinks about all the things he has seen and done that day:

Aa
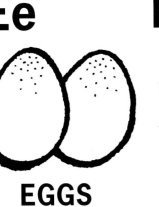
APPLE

Bb

BIRD

Cc

CAT

Dd

DOG

Ee

EGGS

Ff

FROG

Gg

GATE

Hh

HILL

Ii

INSECT

Jj
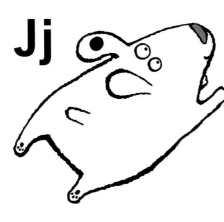
JUMP

Kk
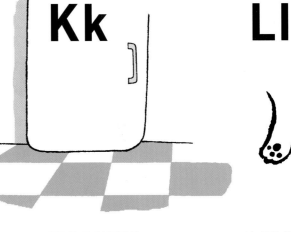
KITCHEN

Ll
LEGS

Mm

MEAL

Nn

NOSE

Oo

ORANGE

Pp

POND

Qq

QUACK

Rr

RAIN

Ss

SKY

Tt

TREE

Uu

UMBRELLA

Vv

VICKY

Ww

WATER

Xx

E<u>X</u>TREMELY

Yy

YAWN

Dog curls up in his basket and falls fast asleep before he can even think of the last letter of the alphabet.

ZZZZZZzzzzzzzzzz

Zz